The Ugly Duckling

Story by:
Hans Christian Ander...

Adapted by:
Margaret Ann Hughes

Illustrated by:
Russell Hicks
Douglas McCarthy
Theresa Mazurek
Allyn Conley-Gorniak
Julie Ann Armstrong

This Book Belongs To:

Use this symbol to match book and cassette.

nce upon a time, on a beautiful warm summer morning, in a rushy thicket near a pond, a mother duck sat on her six eggs. Father Duck waited anxiously nearby.

For days the mother duck sat on her eggs, keeping them warm and toasty. Until finally, one day, the eggs began to hatch.

The father and mother duck watched as the eggs broke open, one by one; and one by one the little ducks appeared… all but the last little one.

But no matter how hard they tried to coax the baby duck out of the egg, that last and biggest egg just would not hatch.

Now the little pond, with its surrounding banks, was the home of many animals. Among them were four families of ducks, two geese, two swans, a beaver, and lots of fish. On the other side of the pond lived a family of toads.

Meanwhile, the mother duck still sat patiently on her egg until…finally, the moment came when the last egg started to hatch.

Now by this time, all the animals had heard about the last egg that would not hatch. So, when the mother duck started shouting, they raced to the nest to see the new baby duckling.

The egg cracked open, and very slowly a dark gray, not-so-tiny duck appeared.

The father duck squeezed past the other animals to get a good look at the new baby, Hector.

All the animals laughed at Hector. He didn't look exactly like the other baby ducks. As the animals teased, tears rolled down the little duckling's cheeks.

Hector buried himself deep into his mother's chest feathers.

The beaver, the geese, and all the other animals walked away laughing, leaving Hector and his family alone. Hector stayed close to his mother, doing his best to hide beneath her large soft wings.

Just then, two beautiful white swans glided past. Hector wanted to be beautiful, too.

During the next few days, the animals of the pond teased Hector whenever they saw him, and even though his parents tried to comfort him, Hector still felt very bad.

Then one night, when everyone was fast asleep in the thicket, the little duckling decided to run away. He quietly tiptoed into the night.

Hector waddled along the edge of the pond. It was getting dark, and the evenings were turning cold. Fall was coming. As Hector waddled along, he heard hoots and whistles, and scary noises. The night sounds frightened him. He stopped and hid beneath a thick hedge along the pond.

And while the moon danced on the night dew all around him, Hector fell asleep.

When Hector awoke the next morning, he continued to run away from home. As he made his way along the bank of the pond, a large green toad suddenly jumped in front of Hector.

The toad stopped jumping and came to rest in front

of Hector. He introduced himself. His name was Otis.

Hector explained that he was running away because the other animals teased him for being ugly.

Otis did a wonderful thing. He told Hector that true beauty isn't what you are on the outside–it's what you are on the inside, by the things you do and say. Hector started feeling a lot better about himself.

Otis convinced Hector to go back home and face things with a positive outlook.

Hector waved good-bye to Otis with his little stubby wing and swam home just as fast as he could.

When he reached the thicket, his family came
swimming out to meet him. They were all happy
he was home.

Winter was coming. The geese, the swans, and
the other ducks were flying south for the winter.
To protect Hector from all the teasing that
might happen along the way,

Mother and Father Duck decided not to go south,
but to keep the family home that winter.

Then winter came. The pond froze over with ice, and snow gently fell on the thicket. Hector and his family stayed inside to keep warm.

Finally, after a long winter…spring came. The sun showered the little thicket with warmth. The icy pond melted and the snow disappeared. Just then there was a loud flapping noise in the sky. Hector's brothers and sisters quickly ran out of the thicket to the pond and saw all the other ducks, geese and swans returning from the south. Each bird landed on the pond, one after the other.

But Hector wouldn't come out of the thicket. He just
knew all the other animals would start laughing at
him again, and that's what he had been dreading all
winter long. He just wasn't ready to face them again.

Everyone called to Hector to come and join them in
a swim. But Hector wasn't convinced. But then he
started thinking about the things Otis had said.

With Otis' song in his heart and his head held high,
Hector left the thicket and swam out onto the
pond…to face the world.

Hector looked down at his reflection in the water.

When he saw himself in the pond, he didn't see an ugly duckling staring back at him. Instead, he saw a beautiful white bird with soft white feathers and a long slender neck.

Oh what a wonderful story! Hector was a lovely swan!! And although the duck family never found out how a swan egg got into their nest to begin with, they loved Hector just like one of their own and took good care of him. Hector had learned from Otis that things don't get better by running away or hiding and about the true beauty that comes from inside.

You see, even though nature made Hector into a beautiful swan, it was the kindness within Hector that made him truly beautiful.

 nd they all lived happily ever after.